Connie Sharar

photographs by Dennis Mosner

Dutton Children's Books ❖ New York

Afghan Angel

Bb

Beagle Baking

Cc

Chihuahuas Cha-cha-cha-ing

Dd

Dachshund Driving

Ee

Entertaining English Pointer

Ff

Flying French Bulldog

Gg

Glamorous Golden Retriever

Hound Hurrying

Intelligent Irish Setter

Jumping Jack Russell

Keeshond King

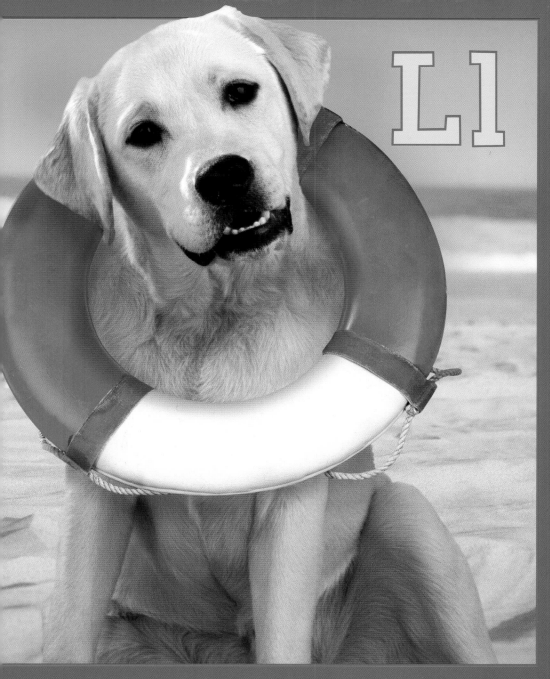

L1

Labrador Lifeguard

Mm

Movie Star Mutt

Norwich Newsie

Oo

Outstanding Old English Sheepd[og]

Pp

Poodle Police Dog

Qq

Queenly Queensland Heeler

Rr

Rottweilers Rafting

Ss

Shepherd Santa

Tt

Trick-or-Treat Terrier

Uu

Ultimate Underdog

Vv

Vizsla Vanishing

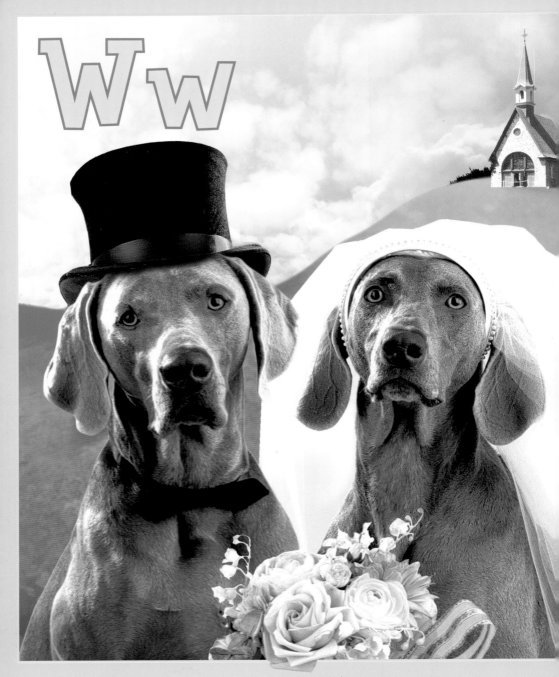

Weimaraner Wedding

Xx

Xoloitzcuintle Xylophonist

Yoga Yorkie

Zero dog breeds begin with the letter Z.

Tell us one and we'll take you to tea!

for Griffin, the puppycat

Thanks to my husband, Robert Conway, for his encouragement and many gifts.
This book was created with the help of many talented people, including
Dennis Mosner, Tucker Hartshorne, Stephanie Garcia, Rob Houston,
and all the ABC Dogs and their owners. Thank you.

Special thanks to Alissa Heyman and Laura Blake Peterson

CIP Data is available.

Published in the United States 2003 by Dutton Children's Books,
a division of Penguin Young Readers Group
345 Hudson Street, New York, New York 10014
www.penguin.com

Manufactured in China
ISBN 0-525-47150-2
First Edition
1 3 5 7 9 10 8 6 4 2